The Fairies of
Starshine Meadow

Rose and the
Perfect Pet

The Fairies of Starshine Meadow

Rose and the Perfect Pet

Kate Bloom and Emma Pack

Fairy Lore
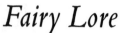

In Starshine Meadow, a grassy dell,
Shimmering fairies flutter and dwell.
Throughout the seasons they nurture and nourish,
Helping the plants and flowers to flourish.

To grant humans' wishes is the fairies' delight,
Spreading magic and happiness in day- and moonlight.
But to human beings they must remain unseen,
So says their ruler, the Dandelion Queen.

When a wish has been made the fairies must speed,
Back to the meadow to start their good deed.
There they must seek the queen's permission,
Before setting off on their wish-granting mission.

And when the queen has agreed, wait they must,
For a sprinkling of her special wish-dust.
Then off they fly to help those who call,
Spreading their magic to one and all.

When a wish is made and fairies are near,
You can be certain that they will hear.
They'll work their magic to make a dream come true,
And leave a special fairy charm just for you!

For fairies love the secret work they do,
And a fairy promise is always true.
So next time you're lonely or full of woe,
Call on the fairies of Starshine Meadow!

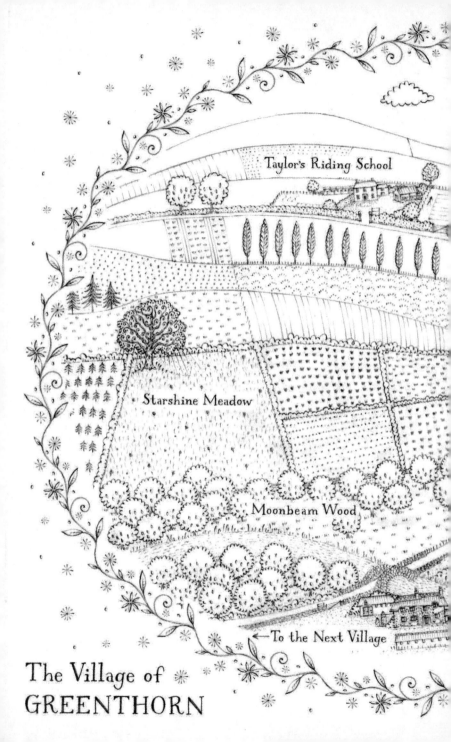

Taylor's Riding School

Starshine Meadow

Moonbeam Wood

←To the Next Village

The Village of
GREENTHORN

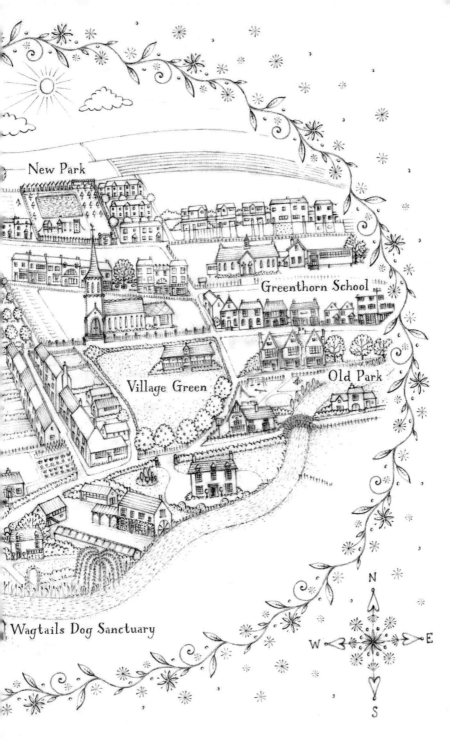

To Graham, who lights up my life.
KB

With love and thanks to the 'original' May and George.
EP

STRIPES PUBLISHING
An imprint of Magi Publications
1 The Coda Centre, 189 Munster Road, London SW6 6AW

A paperback original
First published in Great Britain in 2006

Characters created by Emma Pack
Text copyright © Susan Bentley, 2006
Illustrations copyright © Emma Pack, 2006
With thanks to Gail Yerrill

The right of Emma Pack and Susan Bentley to be identified as the originator
and author of this work respectively has been asserted by them in accordance
with the Copyright, Designs and Patents Act, 1988.

ISBN-10: 1-84715-002-0
ISBN-13: 978-1-84715-002-8

A CIP catalogue record for this book is available from the British Library.

Printed and bound in Belgium by Proost

2 4 6 8 10 9 7 5 3 1

$\mathcal{C}hapter\ \mathcal{O}ne$

Rose fluttered down into the oak's branches, her sparkly pink wings flashing in the autumn sunlight.

"Oh!" she gasped, as a gust of autumn breeze almost blew her into the air again. Her rose-petal skirts and light brown hair streamed out behind her as she clung on to a twig to steady herself.

Hundreds of fairies were gathered in the branches of the great oak in the corner of Starshine Meadow. The tree was home to the Dandelion Queen, and she had called all the fairies together to hear a special announcement.

"There you are, Rose!" called a breathless voice.

With a flash of bright green light, a fairy grabbed the twig next to Rose. She had sparkly green wings and long red plaits. Her flowing green dress was made of tiny ivy leaves.

"Ivy!" Rose beamed at her friend.

"I've been trying to catch up with you!" said Ivy. "Phew! It's hard to fly straight in this breeze, isn't it?"

"Yes!" Rose pushed her hair out of her eyes. "Do you know where Belle and Daisy are?"

"I think they're on their way," said Ivy. "I'm sure they'll find us."

"Hush!" said a nearby fairy. "Here comes the queen."

A sound of tinkling bells came from inside the tree as the Dandelion Queen appeared, wearing a golden petal gown. Her silver blonde curls floated out under her crown.

"Fairies!" said the Dandelion Queen. "I have gathered you here to ask for your help. I am making a wonderful dream-dust and it needs a special perfume, so that when it is used on human beings the gorgeous smell will make them relax and have wonderful dreams."

"Dream-dust. What a wonderful idea!" Rose sighed. One of her favourite things was daydreaming.

"I'd like each group of fairies to work together to make a perfume. There will be a prize for the most delicious scent," the queen explained.

"How exciting!" Ivy whispered.

"The perfumes must be ready by the new moon, in four days' time," said the queen. "Good luck!"

The fairies flew away, chatting excitedly and eager to get started.

Rose smiled at her friend. "Shall we go and look for Belle and—"

Suddenly, there was a flash of mixed blue and yellow light as two fairies whooshed straight down through the branches and landed next to Rose and Ivy.

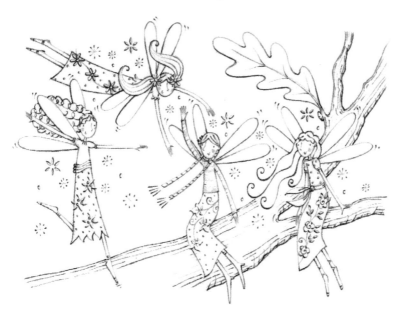

Bluebell folded her sparkling blue wings and swayed gently in the wind, her dark hair streaming behind her. "Rose! Ivy! We thought we'd never find you!" she said. "Daisy and I were blown right up to the top of the tree."

"And now we've been blown down again! Windy weather is such fun!" said Daisy, fluttering her bright yellow wings and doing a somersault. Her pink-tipped, daisy-petal skirt fanned out around her legs and her blonde bunches bobbed up and down.

Rose, Bluebell and Ivy laughed.

"Now we're all together, we can start making plans for our perfume," said Rose.

"I know – we could make bluebell-water!" said Bluebell.

"Or daisy-water?" Daisy suggested.

"Ivy flowers have a nice smell too," said Ivy.

"I thought we could make rose-water," said Rose. "After all, roses have the best scent of all."

Ivy, Daisy and Bluebell nodded. "That's true," they agreed, trying hard not to sound disappointed.

"Maybe we could start with some rose petals and then add all kinds of other lovely smelly things," suggested Daisy.

"Like what?" said Rose.

"Oh, I don't know yet! But I'm bound to think of some other delicious smelling things!" Daisy sang out. "The perfume's going to be gorgeous!"

The others gave Daisy anxious looks. Her madcap ideas often got out of hand!

"Why don't we start by collecting some rose petals?" Rose said quickly, before a squabble broke out. "There's a garden on the far side of Greenthorn with lots of beautiful rose bushes. Anyone coming?"

She flew into the meadow, skimming low over the grass. And with a whirring of fairy wings, Ivy, Bluebell and Daisy flew after her.

The fairies whizzed over the fence, up the overgrown lane and sped towards Greenthorn. Flying high above the shops and rows of neat houses, they soon came to the far side of the village.

"That's the one!" Rose said, pointing towards the very last house in the village. It had red brick walls and a big back garden.

As the fairies swooped down over the garden, a delicious smell of roses wafted up on the breeze.

Rose stopped so suddenly that Daisy almost banged into her. "Can you smell that? And have you ever seen so many gorgeous roses in one garden?" she said, drifting down to land in a bush of dark-red roses which had been planted close to a window at the back of the house.

Ivy, Belle and Daisy flew down beside her.

"You're right," said Ivy, admiringly. "The roses do smell lovely. And their petals look so velvety and soft."

Rose smiled, and was just wondering how to collect the petals when – through the open window – she saw a girl come into the room.

"Quick! Hide!" she said urgently. She shot behind one of the roses and the others quickly joined her.

It was an important fairy law that fairies must never be seen by humans. The Dandelion Queen was very unhappy with any fairy who broke this rule, even if it was by accident. She had to make some special magic dust to sprinkle on the human, so they forgot everything they had seen.

The fairies watched from their hiding place as a man and a woman followed the girl into the room.

"Fancy you reading your poem out at assembly. What a clever-clogs you are, Neema Chopra," the man said with a smile. He was tall, with brown hair and glasses.

"I was a bit nervous at first," Neema said to her dad. "But everyone loved it. They all clapped like mad when I'd finished!" The girl looked about eight and had an oval face and two beautiful black plaits.

"She looks really nice, doesn't she?" Rose whispered.

The other fairies nodded.

"What's your poem about?" asked Neema's mum.

Neema bit her lip. "Er ... about wanting a dog," she murmured.

Mrs Chopra laughed. "I might have guessed! Let's hear it, then!"

As Neema nodded, Rose leaned forward eagerly. She loved writing poetry and was always collecting interesting words.

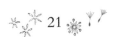

Neema took a deep breath and started to read...

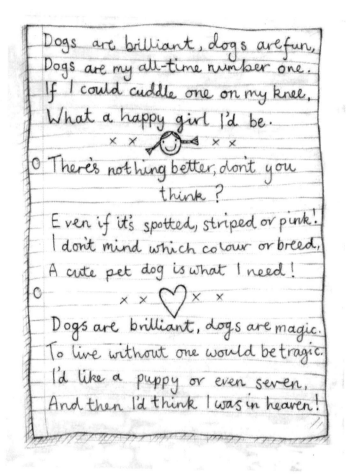

Dogs are brilliant, dogs are fun,
Dogs are my all-time number one.
If I could cuddle one on my knee,
What a happy girl I'd be.

There's nothing better, don't you think?

Even if it's spotted, striped or pink!
I don't mind which colour or breed,
A cute pet dog is what I need!

Dogs are brilliant, dogs are magic.
To live without one would be tragic.
I'd like a puppy or even seven,
And then I'd think I was in heaven!

Neema's parents clapped with delight. "That's brilliant," said her mum, giving her daughter a cuddle.

Rose only just stopped herself from clapping too. "Neema's great at writing poems, isn't she?" she whispered.

"Almost as good as you!" Daisy replied cheekily.

Neema's green eyes sparkled. "So, can I have a dog then?" she asked. "I promise I'll look after it."

Mrs Chopra sighed. "Oh, Neema, you know the answer to that. We're all out of the house during the day and it wouldn't be fair on a dog. Besides, your dad wouldn't want a puppy digging up his prize roses, would he?"

Mr Chopra frowned. "Definitely not!" he said. "I'm sorry, Neema. A dog's out of the question. It's just not practical."

Neema's bottom lip trembled. She pulled away from her mum and ran out into the garden, still clutching her poem.

"Neema? Where are you going?"

called her mum, hurrying after her.

Neema sat down out of sight,
behind the rose bush where the fairies
were hiding. "It's not fair. I want a
dog more than anything!" she cried,
a tear running down her face.

Rose's tiny heart went out to Neema. "If only there was something I could do," she sighed.

Neema wiped her eyes. "I wish…"

Time seemed to stand still. Rose glanced across at her friends who were all watching, wide-eyed. Rose could hardly contain her excitement as she turned back to look at Neema.

Something really special was about to happen.

Chapter Two

"I wish … I could somehow have a dog," Neema said, gazing down at her poem.

Rose watched delightedly, as a little cloud of sparkling silvery mist appeared above Neema's head. Letters formed out of the mist and the wish-words hung there as plain as the black spots on a ladybird.

Rose opened and closed her wings in excitement and only just managed to stop herself from fluttering right out of the bush. Now she could help Neema!

"Don't worry, Neema, I'm going to make your wish come true!" Rose promised.

"There you are," called Neema's mum as Neema stood up. "I'm really sorry you can't have a dog, but it's just not possible. Now come inside and I'll make your favourite tea – beans on toast with melted cheese."

As soon as Neema and her mum were back inside the house, all the fairies flew out of the rose bush.

"You've got a wish!" Daisy exclaimed. "How exciting!"

"Congratulations!" said Bluebell. "We'll help you collect it and take it to the Dandelion Queen."

"Thank you," said Rose, taking a spider-silk net from her bag. "We need to pick a few rose petals too, but I'm so excited I'm all fingers and thumbs."

Holding one corner of the net each, the fairies gathered up the sparkling letters and rose petals.

Rose flashed into the air and led the way back to Starshine Meadow. As they flew over the fence, a sound like a silvery bell was already ringing from inside the oak.

"Listen!" said Bluebell excitedly. "It's the Dandelion Queen's magic clock. We'd better hurry! Quick Rose, remember your wand!"

Rose fetched her wand and then the fairies flew over to the great tree, with its thick twisted trunk and enormous spreading branches. Every leaf on the tree glowed with magical fairy light, but to human beings it looked just like sunlight shining through the branches.

A lot of other fairies had already clustered along the oak's lower branches, waiting to see who was going to claim the wish.

Daisy swooped down to land on a narrow branch and Ivy and Bluebell squeezed in next to her. "Good luck, Rose!" they called.

Feeling a little anxious, Rose flew down and landed in front of the tiny arch in the trunk.

A final bell-like chime rang out and the Dandelion Queen stepped through the arch.

"Rose! I'm glad to see that you have collected the wish," she said warmly. "Tell me all about it."

"Yes, Your Majesty," Rose replied nervously. "It was made by a girl called Neema Chopra. She has wished to have a dog, but her

parents have said no because there's
no one to look after it."

The queen looked thoughtful.
"It will be a difficult wish to grant as
there are good reasons why Neema
can't have a dog," she said gently.
"This might be quite tricky, Rose."

Rose's heart gave a panicky little
skip. "Oh please, Your Majesty. Let
me grant this wish!" she begged.
"Neema's a lovely girl and she
seemed so upset."

The queen seemed pleased by
Rose's eagerness. "Very well. But
you will have to be especially clever
in finding ways to make Neema's
wish come true without upsetting her
parents. And remember, good magic
always works out for the best, but

not always in the way we expect."

Rose sighed with relief. "I'll remember," she promised.

The queen nodded, satisfied. "Hold out your wand, Rose."

Rose did so. The queen shook her starry dandelion wand and a shower of bright golden wish-dust whooshed towards Rose's wand. It twinkled with the tiniest, delicate dandelion seeds.

"Use this magic well. Its power will start to fade after the new moon, in four days' time," the queen explained.

"Thank you, Your Majesty." Rose held up her wand. The glittering pink star on the end seemed to fizz with new power.

Rose flew into the air and took off across Starshine Meadow, followed by Ivy, Bluebell and Daisy. The other fairies cheered and waved.

"Good luck, Rose!" they called.

Daisy, Ivy and Bluebell caught up with Rose as she hovered above a patch of bright red poppies in the middle of Starshine Meadow. "Have you got any ideas about helping Neema get a dog?" asked Daisy.

"Neema can't have a dog of her own," Rose reminded her. "But I thought I'd see if there were any dogs nearby that she could help with. Maybe she could dog-sit for someone."

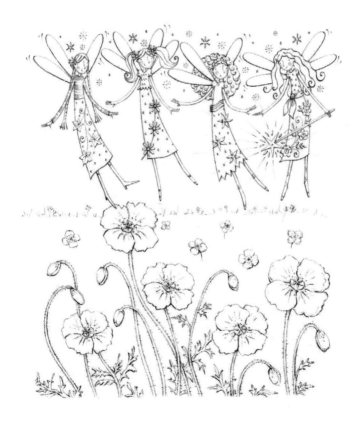

"That's a great idea!" said Ivy. "How are you going to find them?"

"I'm still thinking about that!" Rose replied. "Shall I make a start on the perfume? I often get ideas when my mind's on something else."

Her friends nodded and Rose flew off towards her bed feeling excited and nervous. She had just four days to make Neema happy and there was the perfume to make for the Dandelion Queen's dream-dust, too.

Chapter Three

The following afternoon, Rose was having a lovely daydream while she stirred the tiny pot of rose petals.

She imagined Neema sitting with a little Jack Russell dog on her knee, then somehow it changed to a spaniel chasing a ball, and finally it became a basset hound with long floppy ears!

Rose frowned. The daydream had made her think. There were so many different dogs! She had no idea what kind of dog Neema liked!

"Before I can grant her wish, I have to find out exactly what Neema loves about dogs," she told Ivy, Daisy and Bluebell the moment they fluttered down to her bed. "A tiny cuddly dog's no good if she wants a big bouncy one to play with!"

"How will you find out?" asked Belle.

"Maybe I'll find some clues if I go back to Neema's house," Rose decided.

"And what about the perfume?" asked Daisy excitedly. "How's it coming along?"

Rose peered into the pot. "It's all weak and watery. I don't think it's quite right yet."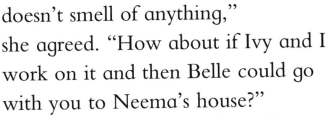

Daisy flew over and had a sniff. "It doesn't smell of anything," she agreed. "How about if Ivy and I work on it and then Belle could go with you to Neema's house?"

"Good idea," said Bluebell.

Rose hesitated for a moment. She really wanted to get the rose-water right, but she also wanted to make a start on granting Neema's wish. She smiled. "That's a good plan. Thanks everyone," she said. "Come on, Belle, let's go!"

As soon as Rose and Belle reached Neema's house, they drifted down on to the window sill near the rose bush and peeped into the sitting room. Neema and her dad were watching a TV gardening show.

"Neema looks really bored," said Bluebell. "I bet she'd rather be watching something about dogs."

"That's it!" said Rose. "You've just given me a great idea, Belle. Follow me!"

Making sure they weren't seen, the fairies flew in through the open window and landed on a table ledge behind the TV.

Rose shook her wand gently and whispered,

Wishes big and wishes small,
With my wand I'll grant them all.
Wish-dust now let Neema see,
Doggy programmes on TV!

There was a bright golden flash and a fountain of sparkly wish-dust shot towards the back of the TV. Rose and Belle flew up and hid behind the curtain to watch.

"Look, the magic's working," said Bluebell.

With a tiny crackle the screen changed from showing gardening to a programme about training puppies.

Neema's face suddenly brightened. "Oh, a programme about dogs. Can we watch this?"

"That's odd,"
said Mr Chopra,
frowning. "I didn't
change the
channel." He pressed
a button on the remote
control and the picture
changed to sheepdog trials.

"Even better!" Neema said.

Mr Chopra tried again, but each
time he pressed a button, dogs
appeared on the screen.

"What's wrong with
this TV? Every single
channel's got dogs on
it!" Eventually he got
up and went out of
the room. "I'm going
back to my roses!"

Rose and Bluebell watched while Neema gazed in delight as the obedient dogs sat on command and walked at heel. When a Labrador was let off its lead to have a runabout with a ball she came and sat on the carpet to watch.

"Yeah! Go for it boy!" Neema cried, clapping her hands. But then her face clouded as she said softly, "I wish I could have a dog like that to play with."

Rose glanced at Bluebell. "So that's the kind of dog Neema wants – one she can take for walks and play with in the park."

Bluebell nodded. "Your TV magic really worked. Now you just have to find a way to help Neema."

"Yes!" Rose said excitedly. "Let's go back and tell the others."

"What's that awful smell?" Rose gasped, screwing up her nose as she fluttered under the wild rose bush. "It's like … wet dog and onions!"

Ivy had a tiny peg on her nose and her face looked green.

Daisy was fluttering around madly, trying to fan the nasty smell away. "Sorry, Rose! The perfume went a bit wrong. It must have been the toadstools I put in it!"

Ivy flew up with the pot of spoiled perfume and tipped it away on to the grass.

Bluebell chuckled. "Never mind, Daisy. We can make some more."

"And maybe skip the toadstools next time?" Rose suggested, spluttering with laughter.

"I will, don't worry," Daisy said, looking serious. "How did you get on with Neema's wish?"

Rose explained about changing the TV channels. "Now I know that Neema wants a dog to run about and play with, I can start looking for someone who needs help with dog-walking. I'm going over to Neema's house tomorrow to see if I can find out whether any dogs live nearby. Which is just as well, as we're going to need more rose petals!"

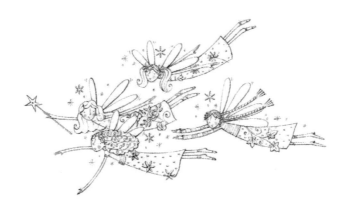

Chapter Four

Grey clouds blew across the sky as Rose and her friends flew over to Greenthorn the following day.

The fairies drifted down into Neema's garden and Ivy, Belle and Daisy landed in a bush of pink roses.

Rose made a wobbly landing on the edge of a birdbath, fluttering her wings quickly to steady herself.

"Are you all right, Rose?" cried Ivy, swooping over.

"It's just so windy!" said Rose, smiling down at her friend's reflection in the water. Suddenly her face lit up. "I've just had a brilliant idea! I can use the water in the birdbath as a magic mirror!"

"What for?" asked Daisy.

"Wait and see!" said Rose, smiling. She took a deep breath.

Wish-dust, wish-dust, help me see,
Where Neema's playful dog might be!

She shook her wand lightly and a fountain of golden wish-dust sprayed over the water. As it swirled around, shapes began forming. All the fairies

leaned over to watch as a picture of
a huge Great Dane appeared,
walking past Neema's front gate.

"Oh, Neema would just love
him!" Daisy enthused.

"Yes. But he's far too big for her to manage!" said Ivy. "Look, the picture's changing."

The fairies watched as a lovely golden Labrador appeared at the door of a house in Neema's street. But just as Rose leaned forward eagerly, three laughing children came running out after their dog. "Oh, that dog would have been perfect, but he's already got lots of people to look after him," she said disappointedly. "Aren't there any dogs who Neema can help?"

"Wait a minute. Look!" said Belle, as dogs of all kinds appeared in big clean pens with comfy beds.

Daisy's eyes widened. "Wow! What gorgeous dogs! And so many!

I wonder where they live?"

"I think we're about to find out," Rose said, as a river and fields appeared, together with some farm buildings. There was a sign outside.

"*Wagtails Dog Sanctuary*," read Rose, excitedly. "Look, it's full of all kinds of dogs. I bet they'd love some extra help. This could be perfect for Neema. I think those fields are next to Moonbeam Wood. Let's go and have a look. We can pick up some rose petals on the way back."

The others nodded and then all together they whooshed upwards on shining wings.

"What an adventure!" said Daisy, excitedly.

Wagtails was almost in the next

village to Greenthorn, in a barn at
the back of a farmhouse. They could
see people cleaning pens and filling
food dishes through the open door.

There were a couple of visitors
looking around, so the fairies were
very careful to slip inside without
being seen. Then they flew from pen
to pen, looking at the dogs.

Ivy hovered near a pen with a

small fluffy white dog. "Oh, what a cute poodle!"

Daisy spotted a big brown and black dog with a bushy tail. "And here's a lovely German shepherd," she said, almost fluttering through the wire mesh. The dog pricked its ears and growled softly. "Um … I'm not sure he's very friendly!" she said, hastily flying backwards.

Suddenly Rose spotted a black and white collie, with gentle dark eyes. He had a tag on his collar with "Dylan" on it. "Oh, you're gorgeous!" she breathed.

Dylan woofed softly and wagged his tail as Rose flew into his pen. "Hello, Dylan. I know someone who would love to meet you."

Ivy, Daisy and Bluebell all flew over and settled in a line on Dylan's back. Dylan turned his head and sniffed gently.

"That tickles!" Daisy said, squealing with laughter just as footsteps sounded out in the corridor.

"Someone's coming!" cried Rose.

The four fairies whizzed out of sight behind Dylan's bed.

A girl wearing a T-shirt and
jeans appeared, carrying a bowl of
dog food. She had short hair and
wore a badge with "Cathy" on it.

"Here you are, Dylan," said Cathy, putting down the food. She stroked Dylan's soft ears. "I bet you'd love a walk, wouldn't you? But we've had so many new dogs in lately I'm rushed off my feet. Sorry, old fella."

She went out and closed the pen door. As soon as Cathy had gone, the fairies fluttered up and hovered in the air above Dylan.

"Wagtails could definitely do with some help," Ivy said.

"Yes," Bluebell agreed. "And I bet Neema would love to take Dylan for walks."

"There are two problems," Rose said. "First, I have to find a way to let Neema know about Wagtails.

And then I have to persuade her
parents to let her come here."

As the fairies flew back towards
the outside door, Daisy spotted a
notice-board. "Look! There's going
to be a fundraising event for
Wagtails this weekend, outside the
supermarket in Greenthorn."

Rose, Ivy and Bluebell gathered round. On the board there was a photo of Cathy with some of the rescue dogs from the sanctuary.

"There's a picture of Dylan!" said Bluebell.

Rose beamed at her friends. "This is just what we need! Somehow we have to make sure Neema and her mum go to the supermarket."

Chapter Five

The following morning, the fairies were busy with their perfume. They gathered round the little pile of fresh rose petals they'd collected from Neema's garden and tried to decide what to do next.

"Maybe we should crush them up this time," Rose said. "Perhaps that will bring out their scent."

"Leave it to me," Daisy said. "I know just what to do. I've got some nettle juice and squashed crab apples to put in this time. It'll smell fabulous, trust me."

Rose glanced doubtfully at Ivy and Bluebell. "Are you sure?"

"Absolutely!" said Daisy.

"Okay, Daisy. But remember, we've only got two days left before the new moon," Rose reminded her.

"Er … right," Daisy said, sounding less confident. "Perhaps you could write a special poem to help make the perfume work? Just in case."

"What a good idea! I'll start on it right away," Rose replied, smiling. "If you're sure you're happy working on the perfume, I'll go and do some thinking about Neema's wish."

Her pink wings sparkled as she flew off. Whizzing under the wild rose bush, Rose lay down on her bed and looked up at the canopy of pink spider-silk. She always got her best ideas when she was relaxing.

Soon she was having the most brilliant daydream about winning the prize for the best perfume. "Thank you so much, Your Majesty," she murmured, performing a graceful curtsy.

"Rose? Are you awake?" said an urgent voice.

"Ivy!" Rose said, sitting up and rubbing her eyes. "I wasn't really asleep. I was thinking!"

Ivy was trying not to laugh. "Have you finished your poem? I think we're going to need it!"

"I haven't had time…" Rose began, but Ivy had already flown up out of the bush. "Hey, wait for me!" she cried.

Rose flew up after her and they made their way to Daisy's bed in a patch of long grass. Some of the fairies were hard at work on their perfumes and sweet smells drifted on the breeze above Starshine Meadow.

Rose fluttered down to Daisy's

bed of yellow spider-silk, where a very odd smell greeted her.

"Peanut butter and bananas?" Rose said, sniffing.

"I know!" Daisy wailed. "I thought I'd just try a tiny bit of bark, but I think it must have been mouldy. I've spoiled the perfume again and used all of the rose petals. Oh, dear. What a disaster! I've let you all down."

"No you haven't!" said Rose firmly, giving her a hug. "You did your best. Besides, you're the kindest, most generous friend anyone could have."

"And we think so too!" said Bluebell and Ivy.

"Really?" Daisy said, smiling.

"Really," said Rose. "Don't worry. We can have another go at the perfume if we go to Neema's house and get more petals. And my poem will be ready by tomorrow."

Daisy gave her friends a watery smile. "Third time lucky?" she said.

"Definitely!" the others chorused!

As the fairies flew towards Neema's house, they passed the busy supermarket. Cathy from Wagtails was outside with a table and some boards covered with more photos of all the dogs. Another girl in a Wagtails T-shirt stood nearby with a collecting tin.

"Wagtails are there already!"
said Rose, forgetting all about rose
petals. "I have to find a way to make
Neema and her mum go shopping!"

"What are you going to do?"
asked Ivy as they quickly flew on.

Rose smiled. She had a great
idea, but it was going to be a surprise.

"Look! There's Neema with her
mum!" said Belle, pointing to two
familiar figures walking along the
high street.

"But they're heading away from
the supermarket," said Daisy.

Taking care not to be seen, Rose
shook her wand and whispered,

Wish-dust, wish-dust, never fail,
Make me a sparkling paw-print trail!

A shower of dust sprinkled the pavement and a line of gleaming paw prints appeared leading towards the supermarket.

"The paw prints are invisible to everyone except Neema," said Rose. "I just need to make her notice them."

Rose flew into a tree just as Neema passed beneath it. She tapped a small branch with her wand and a shower of tiny golden leaves rained down on Neema, landing gently on her head and shoulders.

As she brushed them off, Neema looked down and spotted the glowing paw prints. "Oh, where did they come from? They seem to be leading somewhere. Mum, we have to go this way!" she said, tugging her mum's sleeve.

"Neema's bound to see the Wagtails display now!" said Ivy, clapping her hands. "You're so clever, Rose."

"Neema, where are we going?" asked Mrs Chopra, frowning, as she tried to keep up. "This isn't the way to the library."

But Neema didn't answer. She had spotted the Wagtails display outside the supermarket, and was hurrying towards it.

The fairies quickly flew down to
the display and hid behind a table
leg. They peeped out and saw
Neema pointing to one of the posters
and talking urgently to her mum.

"Now's my chance!" said Rose, waving her wand.

A rush of glittery wish-dust shot towards a photo of Dylan. It began to glow and sparkle with fairy light, visible only to Neema. The photo of Dylan grew extra bright and his eyes seemed to twinkle.

As Neema noticed it, her eyes widened. "Oh," she gasped. "What a gorgeous dog! It's just like his eyes are twinkling at me!" She turned round and called to her mum. "Mum! Come and look at this!"

The fairy magic faded, just as Mrs Chopra came over. "What is it now, Neema?"

"Look at this lovely collie dog. He's called Dylan," Neema said eagerly. "He's just the sort of dog I'd love. Can we go and visit him?"

Mrs Chopra looked at the photo. "I don't know…" she began.

Cathy came over, smiling. "Hello, I'm Cathy. I work at Wagtails. I couldn't help hearing you talking about Dylan."

"He's gorgeous," said Neema.

"Well, you're welcome to visit him any time. He'd love it!"

"Please, Mum," Neema pleaded. "Can we just go and see him?"

"Well, I suppose we might be able to go tomorrow, but I'm not making any promises."

Neema threw her arms round her mum. "Thanks!"

"The magic's working really well," said Daisy.

Rose felt a glow of happiness. "Yes! And I didn't need to persuade Neema's mum to go to Wagtails, Neema did it by herself! She's helping to make her own wish come true! Let's leave her to it for now. We still have to collect some rose petals!"

The next morning, Rose was in a panic. "Oh, dear. The new petals we brought back are covered with morning dew," she said with dismay. In all the excitement, she'd forgotten to put them away before she went to bed. "I'll just have to spread them out to dry and hope for the best," she decided.

She desperately wanted to see how Neema and her mum were getting on, but the perfume still had to be made. Tonight was the new moon, when the Dandelion Queen would choose the best perfume.

Ivy, Daisy and Bluebell fluttered over, just as Rose was checking if the petals were dry.

"Oh how pretty!" Ivy said, admiring the drops of dew on the petals, which sparkled like tiny diamonds in the sun.

Daisy flew down and scooped up a tiny handful of warm dew. "This smells wonderful! You're so clever, Rose! You've made the sweetest smelling perfume!"

Rose looked puzzled.

Bluebell and Ivy flew down beside Daisy and bent over her cupped hands to have a sniff. "You're right. It smells fabulous," said Belle. "Well done, Rose, that was a great idea!"

Rose blushed with pleasure as
she realized what must have
happened. With the sun on them, the
dewdrops had soaked up the rose
petals' scent. She had made rose-
water by accident! "But I wouldn't
have noticed if you hadn't, Daisy!"

Daisy smiled. "I'm just pleased our perfume's ready! It really was third time lucky!"

Bluebell produced a tiny spider-silk bag. "I've got a surprise!" she said, taking out a beautiful perfume bottle. "I made this from a crystal bead from a human being's broken necklace. I hope you like it."

"It's gorgeous," Rose said.

Very carefully, trying not to spill a drop, the fairies scooped up the scented dewdrops in their hands. When the crystal bottle was full,

Bluebell pushed in a stopper made from a carved crab-apple seed.

"What about your poem, Rose? Maybe you should say it anyway, for good luck," Ivy suggested.

Rose nodded.

Pepper blowing on the breeze,
Makes a fairy cough and sneeze.
But flower smells in sun and rain,
Make them smile and laugh again.

We've made a perfume you can keep,
To make you yawn and fall asleep.
The moon will shine with silver beams,
On gentle, sweet and loving dreams!

77

"That was lovely, Rose!" Bluebell enthused.

"Yes it was. You're so clever," said Daisy.

"Thanks everyone," said Rose, pink with pleasure. "Now our perfume's ready, shall we all go to Wagtails? I'm dying to catch up with Neema!"

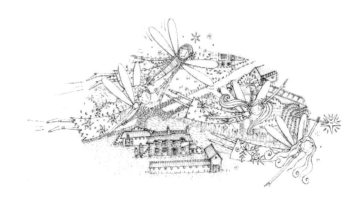

Chapter Six

Saturday mornings were busy at Wagtails. The barn door stood wide open. Making sure they weren't seen, the fairies flew inside and headed straight for Dylan's pen.

Rose felt really excited just imagining the look on Neema's face when she saw Dylan.

But Dylan's pen was empty!

"Oh no!" gasped Daisy. "Maybe he's got a new owner!"

"That would be a good thing, wouldn't it?" asked Bluebell.

"Well – yes," Rose said, trying hard to feel happy. She had been putting all her hopes on Neema and Dylan becoming good friends.

"It's all right, everyone!" said Ivy. "Here's Dylan, and look who's with him!"

Rose turned to look. Neema had Dylan on a lead. She looked proud as punch as she brought him back to his pen. Cathy and Mrs Chopra were walking behind her.

The fairies quickly flew up on to the roof of the pen, where they could watch without being seen.

"Did you enjoy your walk?"
Neema asked Dylan, stroking him.
"Next time I'll bring you a ball.
We're going to have some great
times together."

Dylan woofed softly and wagged his tail.

Cathy smiled at Neema and her mum. "Dylan's going to love having you both visit. He's such a sweet dog. He deserves a good friend."

Mrs Chopra smiled. "Being a dog-walker will do me good. I need the exercise!"

Rose's eyes widened. She could hardly believe her ears. Neema and her mum had offered to help out with dog-walking!

Neema bent down and gave Dylan a hug. "We'll see you again, really soon," she promised.

"It's just a thought," Cathy said to Mrs Chopra, "but we have a pet-fostering scheme. Some people can't have pets because they're out all day during the week, but they can look after a dog at the weekends."

"We could do that!" Neema said quickly. "We're always at home at weekends. Oh, Mum, can we? Please! I'd take care of him."

"Fostering Dylan would be perfect for Neema," Rose whispered. She crossed her fingers and toes, hoping that Neema's mum would agree. If she could have crossed her wings, she would have done that too!

Mrs Chopra hesitated.

Rose, Ivy, Daisy and Bluebell all held their breath.

"It's Sunday tomorrow," Neema said, hopefully. "Can we just give it a try?"

"Why not," Mrs Chopra said, reaching out to stroke Dylan's soft ears. "We'll come over for Dylan in the morning. It will give your dad a chance to meet him!"

"Oh, Mum. Thanks!" Neema said, giving Dylan a huge hug. "Did you hear that Dylan? We're going to foster you."

Dylan woofed again and licked Neema's chin.

Rose's heart swelled with happiness. She could hardly believe it. Neema's wish was coming true in a most unexpected way – just as the Dandelion Queen said it might!

The light of the new moon spread a silver glow over Starshine Meadow and sparkled on the wings of the fairies gathering at the oak. Rose, Ivy, Daisy and Bluebell flew on to a branch near the tiny arch. Rose held the perfume in its twinkling crystal bottle. All the groups of fairies had brought their perfumes and everyone waited excitedly to hear the result of the competition.

With a tinkling of fairy bells the queen appeared in her magnificent flowing gown and silvery crown.

"Greetings, fairies!" she said warmly. "I've smelt some delicious smells all over the meadow. I can't wait to try your perfumes!"

Fairies flew down from the branches, and the queen tried each of the perfumes in turn. "Lily-water, orange-blossom scent, lilac-flower perfume – lovely," she said.

Rose was the last one to step forward. She handed the rose-water to the queen and waited nervously for her to try it.

"How are you getting on with Neema's wish?" asked the queen, with her hand on the bottle's stopper.

"Very well, thank you, Your Majesty," Rose said. She told the queen about Wagtails and how Neema and her parents were going to foster Dylan.

"That's wonderful!" the queen exclaimed. "You've done really well, Rose. It was a difficult wish, but you have helped make Neema very happy." She smiled kindly. "Don't forget, the wish-dust will begin to lose its power soon."

"I won't, Your Majesty," Rose answered, feeling pleased for Neema. There was one last thing she needed to do tomorrow, and Belle, Ivy and Daisy were going to help her.

As the queen opened the perfume bottle, a cloud of the sweetest rose perfume filled the air. "Oh, this is wonderful!" she said, taking a sniff. "Just perfect for my dream-dust. Rose, Ivy, Belle and Daisy – you have won the competition!"

All the fairies clapped.
"Congratulations!" they called.

"And now for the prizes," the
queen said. Four of her fairy helpers
flew over with parcels wrapped in
tiny violet petals.

They gave Rose, Ivy, Daisy and Bluebell a parcel each. As Rose opened her parcel she gasped. "Oh, it's beautiful!" she said, holding up a pink spider-silk gown sewn with tiny velvet rosebuds.

Ivy's gown was green with silver embroidery; Daisy's was yellow with embroidered pearl petals; and Belle's was blue with tiny mauve stars.

"Thank you, Your Majesty," they chorused, happily.

"I can't wait to try mine on," said Daisy, dashing off.

As Rose flew off to her bed with her prize, she felt tired but very happy. She hung up her gown and was asleep the moment her head touched her rose-petal pillow.

The next morning Rose's wings quivered with excitement as she flew over to Neema's house with her three friends.

"There's Neema and Dylan!" Rose exclaimed, drifting down into a bush of white roses.

"And look what a great time they're having," Ivy said.

Neema was throwing a ball and Dylan kept jumping on it and play-growling, making Neema laugh.

Neema's dad came out of the house and walked across the lawn. Dylan bounded up to him. Mr Chopra smiled and stroked him. "I'm glad you persuaded us to foster a dog. Dylan's great."

Neema beamed at her dad. "I'm glad too. He's magic!"

The fairies smiled gleefully. "If only Neema knew!" whispered Rose, from their hiding place.

When Mr Chopra had gone back into the house, Neema sat on the grass with Dylan beside her.

Dylan laid his head on her knee as she stroked his thick black and white fur. "I love having you for a friend," Neema said with a fond smile.

Rose felt very happy. There was just one thing left to do – leave a special fairy charm.

Ivy, Daisy and Belle helped Rose find a big rose petal. Then all together they whispered,

Fairies all will make a charm,
To bring good luck and do no harm!

Rose shook her wand. There was a gold flash and a final shower of sparkly wish-dust whooshed out and covered the petal. All the fairies blew gently on to the dust and tiny writing appeared in glittery gold letters.

Moon bright and moon glow
This we tell, so you will know.
A fairy promise comes your way,
To bring good luck with every day.
For close to you, we're always been,
The best of friends, although unseen.

Holding the petal between them, the fairies flew behind Neema and dropped it gently on to Dylan's back. They had only just zoomed back into the safety of the rose bush when Neema noticed it.

"What's this?" she gasped, as the petal fluttered on to the grass. Her eyes widened as she picked it up and read the poem aloud, running her fingers over the tiny glittering writing.

The moment she had finished, the petal flew out of her hands and dissolved in a burst of golden dust.

"Maybe fairies are real!" she whispered, looking all around. "Wherever you are, thank you for making my wish come true!"

Dylan looked towards the rose bush, where four pairs of tiny shining eyes were watching. He gave a gentle woof of happiness and wagged his tail.